D0147357

Life Before Damaged Vol. 2
The Ferro Family

By:

H.M. Ward

HWM Press

www.SexyAwesomeBooks.com

COPYRIGHT

This book is a work of fiction. Names, characters, places, and incidents are either the product of the author's imagination or are used fictitiously, and any resemblance to actual persons, living or dead, events, or locales is entirely coincidental.

H.M. WARD PRESS
First Edition: December 2014
ISBN: 9781630350529

Life Before Damaged Vol. 2

ODE TO SUCKAGE

GINA

JULY 1ST, 9:02 am

Mondays suck.

Scratch that. Mondays after committing a crime, lying to everyone I love, nearly being charred to a crisp, being tortured by the most beautiful player in the world, and then being rejected by him—that is suckage of the worst kind. Thankfully, that's not my typical weekend MO. I'm too cool for that. Or too lame? Oh, I don't care, I'm just glad it's over!

After Pete left me alone in his study, practically climbing the drapes with desire, one of Pete's servants brought in my freshly cleaned clothes. They returned wrapped in cream-colored tissue paper, tied with a blue satin ribbon, and stamped with the golden seal of the Ferro family crest.

It was like getting a present. I've only seen swank hotels do that. My family has money, but the Ferros seem to have more money than God. I rubbed the pad of my finger over the golden Ferro crest, enjoying the way the texture felt on my skin. I bet it was gold leaf. Nothing's too good for Ferro underpants.

Still fondling the package, the intercom buzzed, scaring me half to death. "Your car is ready, miss. Come down when you're ready."

"All right. I'll be down in five." Before I could say thanks, the intercom cut off and I was alone again.

Pete didn't come back to his rooms. He didn't explain his sudden one-eighty. It's been driving me nuts ever since. I tore the tissue paper and pulled out my clothes. While tugging my blouse over my head, I caught Pete's scent. Who has custom laundry detergent? Oh, God, I was going to smell like him. For a brief moment, I wondered if I should frame the shirt or burn it.

Before leaving the mansion through the back door to Pete's suites, I glanced in the mirror. There was no sign of distress on my clothing, no smoky smell to indicate where I was that night. For a moment, I was thankful. Okay, it was more than that. I'd be dead if it weren't for Pete, so no matter what made him run off, I couldn't be mad. Besides, I'm dating someone and players aren't my type.

Pete's chauffeur drove me to Erin's apartment, where she grilled me relentlessly, asking questions that I couldn't answer. Finally, she gave up and fell asleep on the table, her face in a plate full of Cheetos.

I'm thankful I didn't have sex with Pete. I honestly don't think I could look at myself in the mirror had I gone through with it. I'm already overwhelmed by guilt over my lusty thoughts and can only barely handle the memory of his lips on my neck.

Besides, I have to face Anthony and tell him what happened. I keep trying to blame my lascivious behavior on the state of shock brought on by the traumatic events, but my conscience knows better. I should come clean. I can't have this cloud of guilt hovering over my head all the time. If the roles were reversed I'd want to know, right?

Maybe this will be a good opportunity for us to talk about bringing a little bit more passion into our love life. God knows I wouldn't mind. Starfishing wasn't that far off. Sometimes I need more than gentle. I need to feel like I'm his. I need to feel desired. Right now, our sex life feels more like an experiment than an emotion, "Hey! What do you think will happen if I stick this peg into that hole?" It's not sexy.

In contrast, Pete Ferro is a modern Don Juan. Seduction is a game to him, and he loves playing. Pete knows women, he understands them, and, as a result, women are drawn to him. The man is catnip.

I admit I fell for it, too. In the moment, it felt real, as if we had a connection. I thought being with a player would make me feel dirty, like a conquest or something, but it doesn't feel that way at all. Every second feels heated and passionate, making me want to touch him, to taste his lips. I don't hand out kisses freely. A kiss has to be earned. I don't toss them away like tissues. I guess that's what's bugging me. It seemed real, from Pete's smooth voice whispering poetry, to the way he stormed off at the end, but it wasn't.

Maybe it felt real for him, too; he just didn't realize it until the end.

I laugh at myself. *Keep dreaming, Gina. Pete's a player and always will be.*

But calling him a player doesn't explain why he bolted. I went from feeling like a goddess to feeling like nothing in seconds. Poof! The illusion should have shattered, right? Yet here I am, still lost in it.

I feel so embarrassed by the whole situation. I got played by a player and broke a cardinal rule—whether we actually had sex or not, I wanted to. That's still cheating. I can't believe I moaned in front of him! Hopefully, our paths won't cross again for a long time, and I can put this whole mortifying situation behind me.

Have I said that Mondays suck?

Sleep has been—how to phrase it—*interesting* since Friday night. The few hours of sleep I manage to get are plagued with vivid nightmares combining horror and eroticism into one gigantic ball of angst. I wake up a sweaty, trembling mess.

I see people burning—their bodies literally on fire—crying and screaming out in pain. Their arms reach for me, while their voices call for my help. I try to help them, but I can't get close enough. I stumble through the smoke, panicked, unable to see. My lungs start to burn and I fall to the floor, clawing at the wooden boards until my hands bleed. The smoke swirls, and then I'm naked in Pete's arms. He begins to kiss me, and my heart races in response. The other people begin to cry out again, begging us to help, and Pete tries to race off to save them, but I don't want him to stop. Seduction spills from my lips like poison, deafening Pete to their cries. I sacrifice them all to claim that moment of ecstasy.

No matter how my conscious mind tries to block out the past few hours, my subconscious throws open the door, welcoming the memories. They plague my sleep, drenching me in sweat and causing me to wake screaming. It's getting harder to hide.

Early this morning, I woke the household staff with my screaming, trapped in a nightmare and unable to get out. When my maid, Angelina, finally woke me, she just sat by my bed, watching me with concern in her eyes, but not pushing me to tell her about it. She won't pry, but she knows something is really wrong, she knows something terrifying is keeping me from sleeping. She said she heard me talking, pleading. I have no idea what she heard, but Angelina assured me everything would be fine. I wish that were true, but I'll never be free from the guilt. It will haunt me until the day I die.

GRANZ TEXTILES AREN'T HUNKY-DOREY

10:27 am

I'm sitting at my desk in the Account and Finance Department of Granz Textiles, using a pile of spreadsheets as a pillow. Too bad my desk can't morph into a beast and gobble me up. I imagine desk drawer fangs munching on me in my minds eye. It's cartoonish, and the image makes the corners of my mouth twitch. Damn, I'm crazy. The smoke must have killed off a few of my brain cells.

I need a cappuccino, stat!

Dad offered me a position here for my college internship and I, always the dutiful daughter, accepted without question. As a family, we all decided the best way to establish my place within the family business was to major in finance for my undergraduate degree. It had little to do with my aptitude for numbers.

If I'd had the choice, I'd be working in either product development or design, researching the latest trends and wooing top fashion designers. Being an only child, the company will one day be mine. With that understanding, it is my responsibility to learn all the managerial aspects of the business as quickly as possible. Of course, from my Dad's point of view, having your own flesh and blood tracking the money is an added bonus. It helps ensure the company doesn't get screwed over by any of the staff and board. Who better than your own daughter to make sure every penny is accounted for?

A knock on the door interrupts my working nap, and a perky woman in her early thirties walks into my cubicle holding a stack of papers and files. Charlotte gives me a friendly smile; her auburn curls bouncing, and takes a seat opposite me at the desk. Being the boss's daughter doesn't automatically get you a corner office with a view, but it does get you a very efficient and friendly department assistant.

Every Monday morning, after handing me the latest reports, she fills me in on the office gossip. I love hearing about Charlotte's carefree adventures and her romantic woes; she gets all dreamy-eyed as I describe the various social events I attend. It's a reciprocal case of wanting to know how the other half lives, each a little envious of the other.

I lift my head from the desk, startled, a sheet of paper clinging unattractively to my cheek. I peel it off as nonchalantly as possible and slip it back into its neat stack. Charlotte snorts back a laugh. I manage a small smile, while smoothing a few stray strands of hair back into the tight bun at the nape of my neck and straightening the lapels of my suit jacket.

"Good morning, Charlotte. How was your weekend?"

Charlotte animatedly describes the restaurants she tried, the clubs she danced in, and the men she met. She constantly refers to them as "bachelor number so and so," as if they were contestants on a dating game.

She finishes gushing about bachelor number four and asks, "How about your weekend, honey? Any fancy red carpet events? I feel jealous just imagining it!”

"Nah. My weekend was pretty quiet," I

lie, which is becoming increasingly easier. The thought makes me feel worse. Who am I and what the hell am I doing? Where'd the happy princess go? Nah, that's a lie, too. I was never happy. I was just trapped in a tower, waiting for someone to come bust me out. Apparently I was too impatient, because I burned my castle down.

As per our original plan, I spent the weekend at Erin's apartment under the pretense of helping her with an art project. That way, no one could notice us coming and going to the rave at unusual hours. When news of the warehouse fire went public, my parents called me to let me know. I pretended to be just as shocked as they were. My gut twisted into knots and hasn't let go since. I'm going straight to Hell. There's a pool in the eternal lake of fire with my name on it.

Now I'm stuck with this sick feeling, waiting for the other shoe to drop. My skin is prickling and I jump at every sound. The cops are going to find me and then all Hell will break loose. That is, if I don't confess before that. I don't think I can keep this secret much longer. I refuse to keep my mouth shut if they blame it on someone else.

Erin and I decided it was completely believable to say I hurt myself using a fussy blowtorch while helping with her new piece, a collage of broken glass, tile, and massive amounts of hot glue. Burns, bruising, cuts and scrapes are a continual consequence of Erin's creativity; her hands and arms are always a mess. As for my constant cough? Let's just say that for once I am actually thankful for Erin's chain smoking habit. I always come back from her place wheezy and smelling like the bottom of an ashtray. It's gross but it is the perfect explanation—at least that's what Erin says.

I'm still too mentally vacant to think for

myself. Lame, I know, but I'm not like some web-slinging superhero that can act like nothing happened. I was trapped in a burning building. I could have died—would have died without Pete Ferro there to save me.

I struggle under the weight of my lies. Each additional deceit is like a huge weight added to my aching shoulders. At this rate, I'll look like a hunchback by graduation. I can walk across the stage with my knuckles dragging on the wooden floor.

The thought conjures the warehouse closet, and a phantom stabbing sensation prickles through my nail beds. I feel like I licked a light socket, and my heart rate shoots through the roof. I laugh to cover it, to hide the way my voice will shake when I answer her.

"I spent the weekend hanging out at Erin's apartment, an activity my parents would rather not hear about. We can just skip it." And we'll skip the Pete Ferro part, too, and his luscious man scent. A smile tugs at my lips remembering it, and how much he likes his body-wash.

Looking disappointed by my lack of juicy gossip, Charlotte stands to drop a stack of files on my desk, and misses the dopey grin on my face. "That's too bad. I was looking forward to hearing more about that dreamboat doctor of yours." She lets out a wistful sigh and bats her eyelashes dramatically while pretending to melt. "But it's nice of you to help your friend with her project. Anyway, here are your reports. I need to get back to my desk, the phone is ringing off the hook this morning because of… well, you know. Oh, by the way, your father would like to see you in his office when you have a moment."

"Thank you, Charlotte. You're the best." I smile at her as she exits my cubicle, waving her goodbyes as she walks.

My father.

This whole fiasco has been hard on him. I fell asleep late last night to the sounds of him yelling on the phone in his study. When I came down for breakfast this morning, Mom told me he'd already left for the office.

Another tidal wave of remorse hits me hard. Daddy has to keep his stress under control. His doctor has warned him that his heart can't take more abuse. What if this brings on another heart attack? Dad is already high-strung, and has more than he can handle on his plate. Something like this could easily push him into another attack if he can't expel his stress. I've caused this, and I can't figure out how to help him, how to fix it.

My head falls back on my desk with a thud. I don't even know who I am, what I'm capable of, or what I'll do when push comes to shove. I'm weak, a follower. I'm not this woman who's been tapping the inside of my skull, fighting for control of my mouth. She wants to spurt the truth and damn the consequences. That's not me, so I push her to the back of my brain. Freud would have called her my Id, but she's more of a bitch than anything else.

She's also the one who kept you alive the other night—her and Peter. I shake the thought away.

"Great, now I'm arguing with myself." I don't want to face my dad, but the quicker I get this over with, the sooner I can go back to my numbers and lose myself in work. "Rip off the Band-Aid. Walk in there and spill your guts, Gina." I try to pump myself up, but volunteering to get my head ripped off isn't exactly the kind of thing I want to do today.

As I approach his office, I hear Dad's deep angry voice booming through the walls. When I hear the topic of discussion, I stop in my tracks.

"I want names! Is there any way to accelerate the investigation? Detective, I want the identities of every single person responsible. Assure me you've started arresting people!"

Detective? I swallow a big lump in my throat, realizing he's talking to the police. The lump gets bigger when I hear a real voice answer him. Crap, he's not on the phone. The police officer is here, in his office. I try to stay my trembling hands, but it's impossible.

"We haven't made any arrests yet. The people in charge of the rave were obviously professionals, Mr. Granz. As soon as the fire started, they most likely disappeared from the scene. They left their equipment behind, but the serial numbers have been removed. There is no evidence to link back to them—not even a fingerprint."

Daddy gets more irate. "What do you mean there's no way to find them? Are you telling me they're ghosts? That's bullshit!"

The detective's voice is careful. "Oh, we'll find them. I guarantee you I won't stop until we do. The process of interrogating witnesses has begun, and we've already spoken with the people that were taken to the ER. Some names are coming out, and we are making progress. Some personal items were left scattered in the debris. We'll analyze them and attempt to discover the identities of other people present. If you can provide us with a list of current and past employees, we will cross-reference the lists and see if we can find out who gave them access to your facilities."

For once, being a shy, socially awkward unknown has its privileges. Thank God no one there knew me aside from Erin... and Pete. Shit! Why did I give him my real name? He's a Ferro and can't be trusted. Damn, damn, damn!

"Of course. You have my complete

cooperation, but as soon as you have names, I want to know. I need to know who is responsible, and I want them to pay for this! Do you have any idea what this scandal will do to my company, to my family? I want the people involved, especially the person who let them inside, punished to the full extent of the law. And I can promise you they will have to deal with me in court as well. I'm not going to let some social deviant ruin my family over a goddamn party!"

"I understand completely, Mr. Granz. The information we have at the moment can't be divulged, yet. One of the witnesses is still in a coma and considered to be in critical condition. If this person wakes up, we will see if he can corroborate what we already know. If... well, if he doesn't make it, we're looking at involuntary manslaughter and will be dealing with a whole different set of charges. We don't want any of our main suspects to know we are onto them at this time. They might bolt before we have a chance to make any arrests, and most of them have the means to disappear."

I lean against the wall outside Dad's office and stifle a scream with my hands. Someone's in a coma? Oh, my God! Since Saturday morning I've been playing ostrich, keeping my head in the sand and focusing solely on the material damage. Now the words "involuntary manslaughter" keep ringing in my ears, and I can't get them out. I killed someone. Dear God.

I lean forward, grasping my stomach, trying not to dry heave. They'll hear me, and there's no way to explain why I'm lingering in the hallway, puking.

Bitchy Me escapes her exile and forces me to straighten up and slap a smile on my face. She also points out that confiding in Dad is now off limits. I'm on my own.

I hear chairs being pushed back, and Daddy thanking the detective. Before the door opens, I try to look as unaffected as possible, adjusting the collar of my black blazer and flattening the pleats in my tweed pencil skirt. I'm sure my face is as white as a ghost, the blood having drained out of it.

The police officer exits my dad's office. He looks me over once, noticing the way I'm standing too still and the beads of sweat in my hairline. His eyes narrow slightly, but he just nods in my direction without a word, walking down the posh hallway filled with enormous golden frames of Dad's art collection.

The paintings speak volumes to visitors. The Rembrandt says we're wealthy, the Madonna and Child says we're old money, and the final pieces proclaim our stability; we're not going anywhere. The artwork alone is worth millions of dollars. It screams power. The fact that it's in his office, as well as our home, says he's not afraid to show off his wealth. Daddy knows what he wants and what to do to succeed.

I've always enjoyed watching visitors react to seeing Daddy's money displayed on the walls. Their resulting body language says a lot about their character. This detective ignores the paintings and heads directly to the elevator. Money obviously doesn't impress him, and I'd bet displays of power worry him. Some wealthy families think they are above the law. Daddy does not. I hope the detective can see that.

THE FALL OF THE PERFECT PRINCESS

11:14 am

When I'm poised enough to manage it, I knock on the doorjamb and smile. Dad is sitting behind his desk, resting his head in his hands. He's aged visibly over the past few days. Frown lines etch his face and dark circles rim his eyes. I think his thinning brown hair may have more gray mixed in than usual. That's another weight on my shoulders. I wonder how much more I can take before my spine snaps in two.

I take another step forward and clear my throat, alerting him to my presence. He looks up and it takes him a moment to realize it's me. He smiles warmly, like I'm his ray of light during this storm. I can't take it. I want to tell him, but when he looks at me that way, my confession is lost.

"Hey, Princess, have a seat." Dad motions to one of the leather chairs across from him, and I sit down, legs crossed, back straight, fingers wrapped tightly around my knees.

I study the various family pictures he displays on the corner of his desk. There's one of me at age ten, dressed in a tutu and holding my very first pair of pointe shoes. Another photograph shows my parents and me the day I graduated from high school. A third photograph, taken during spring break vacation a few months ago, is of Anthony and me sitting on the deck of Dad's sailboat. The photos are the typical display of a proud father.

"You wanted to see me, Daddy?"

"I did, and thank God you don't have any bad news. Another second with that man and I would have lost it. Kids, Gina—a bunch of deviants are threatening to destroy this family and everything I've worked so hard to achieve." His voice stills and he breathes in slowly, leaning back in his chair. A smile tugs at his lips, crinkling the corners of his eyes.

"I shouldn't trouble you with this, but it's hard. And I'm sure you heard. You have a way of being within earshot when things are dire. I admire that about you. You've grown into the type of woman who defends her family, protects them in good times and bad. I'm proud of you, Gina, no matter what happens next."

He clears his throat and leans forward, placing his thick fingers on his desk.

“Enough sentimentality. You already know how I feel about you and your mother. The reason I called for you is because I need you to do something. I'll be meeting with our insurance company and our lawyers this afternoon, and I want you to sit in on the meeting. Granz Textiles will most likely be sued by some of these hooligans, trying to squeeze money from us for having been victims while on our property."

He says the word "victims" with venom and disgust. I try to swallow the bile in my throat, knowing I am the biggest hooligan in this scenario. I bury every other emotion deep within. I can’t let it show on my face. He thinks so much of me and I messed up so badly. There’s no way to fix this, not now, not ever.

"Listen, Gina, I want to know where we stand before the lawsuits start coming in." Lawsuits with an S, as in *multiple lawsuits.* I close my eyes and the tension shows on my face, I can't hide it anymore. Daddy leans forward and takes my hands. "We can get through anything if we stick together. Remember that."

The words feel like a hot knife, cutting through me in a clean swipe. Feeling gutted, I sit there, mouth gaping. He has no idea I was the one who let them in to the warehouse. I should tell him, spit it out, and then run for Jersey, or the subway. Those are two places Dad will never go.

Say it. Tell him. I open my mouth, but suddenly his smile returns and his old eyes sparkle with life again. I can't do it. I nod and mutter, "Of course, Dad. I'll be there. Anything else?"

"Come to think of it, yes. And this is good news." I crinkle my brow wondering what he's thinking. Dad continues, "Cancel whatever plans you have for tonight. I'm having dinner with Anthony to discuss the details of the testing phase of my new project, and I want you there, too. I doubt you have any objections?" His small smile widens, making his laugh lines crinkle a bit.

This is surprising news. Anthony is scheduled to work night shifts at the hospital for the next couple of weeks. Between work and school, finding time off is difficult for him. The last time I saw him was briefly over lunch—one day last week. Tonight, I get to sit down face-to-face with him and admit what happened with Pete. He has a right to know.

"Of course I'll be there, Dad. Sounds great."

"Wonderful, and I'll email you all the documents for today's meetings. Try to look over them beforehand." Dad straightens his tie and smoothes his suit. I get up and head toward the door, but Dad calls my name. Standing in the doorway, I turn to look at my father.

"It's times like these your mother and I

realize how blessed we are to have a daughter like you. We don't say it often enough, but we love you, Princess. Now stop worrying. We'll get through this."

UNFRIENDLY COMPETITION

6:12 pm

"Good evening." A young waitress with long jet-black hair stands by our table, notepad in hand, with eyes only for Anthony. "My name is Kitty, I'll be your waitress this evening. May I get you anything to drink while you wait for your other guest to arrive?"

"I'll have a glass of your Chardonnay, please." I tell Kitty, but she doesn't respond.

"Make that a bottle, Kitty." Anthony adds, handing the wine menu back to the waitress and giving her a friendly smile.

"Yes, sir." The waitress leans toward the center of the table to light the candle, smiling at Anthony seductively. Her crisp uniform is unbuttoned at the top, awarding him an unobstructed shot of her lacy lingerie-trimmed cleavage. Seriously? Am I invisible? I fake-cough loudly and she reluctantly straightens and heads to the bar to fill our order.

We're seated at a table set for three in one of Daddy's favorite restaurants, still waiting for him to arrive. The soothing atmosphere, with its low lighting, rich colors, and soft jazz music calm my jitters and smooth my waitress-ruffled feathers.

With all the speculation about the fire at the office, I'm grateful for surprise quality time with my boyfriend—even if it means fighting our waitress for his attention. Due to his overbooked schedule, I haven't actually seen Anthony in days. It's a wonder he's here tonight at all, but I'm happy he is. The sight of him is refreshing and grounding; he keeps me normal.

Anthony looks at his watch, then glances around the restaurant. "What time did your father say he'd be here?" He rubbernecks, searching again for my father.

"He should be here any minute," I shrug. "I guess he's running a little bit late, but I don't mind. It gives us time alone." I give him a shy smile and entwine our fingers together, but after a cursory squeeze, Anthony lets go of my hand and fusses with his napkin instead.

Anthony is tall, with a slender build and light features. His blond hair, blue eyes and soon-to-be-a-doctor status, make him a catch for both my father and me. Over the past couple of months, Granz Textiles has been working on developing a line of revolutionary medical-grade fabrics. To hear my father and Anthony brag about it—which they do incessantly—the new line will revolutionize the medical field. The project, and Anthony's close involvement with it and my dad, is how we met.

Dad founded the Granz Scholarship as a one-time opportunity for a student going into their last year of medical school. In exchange for a very generous amount of money to cover tuition and living expenses in that final year, the student would collaborate with the medical division of Granz Textiles during the testing and approval phases of our new line of medical products. The contract comes to term when the FDA officially approves the product. My father was head of the scholarship board, of course, and had final say in who was chosen. Anthony won the scholarship without contest. Needless to say, he was quite taken by Anthony. So much so, that he insisted Anthony become part of our family by pushing us together as a couple. Anthony is a great guy—sweet, respectful, smart, hardworking, dedicated, and handsome—I didn't mind being set up with him. It's a win-win situation for all of us.

Anthony wasn't born into money like I was. His lower social and financial status makes him consciously grateful to my dad for this opportunity—and considerably more attractive to me. I've always expected my dad would have a say in my eventual marriage, but I imagined he would prefer someone wealthy and likely a silver spoon-fed douche-bag-brat. Anthony and I aren't engaged yet, but I wouldn't be surprised if he asked my dad for his blessing soon, a blessing my dad will give without hesitation. I swear those two are inseparable sometimes.

"I'm so surprised you're here," I say. "How did you manage to get the time off?"

"I told the hospital I had an urgent meeting with the scholarship board." He gives me a small wink. "Did you look over the project files your dad sent us today?"

I nod and try to hide my disappointment. I can't blame Anthony for his enthusiasm—this project is all he ever talks about—but I'd hoped to focus on us in these stolen private moments. Is just a little romance asking too much?

"Yes, I did," I say with a sigh, "and I doubt he will like what I have to say about it. It's not feasible. With his proposed production methods, we will run out of funds before the testing phase even gets under way. The alternative you proposed during our last meeting was more cost efficient." I make a frustrated noise. "It doesn't really matter what I think, though, he probably won't listen to me."

Anthony gives me a reassuring smile.

"I'm sure he will. Even if you weren't his

perfect princess, you are brilliant at what you do. He'll listen to you. Together we'll convince him you're right about this." He squeezes my knee under the table, but removes his hand before I can lay my hand over his.

I'm in such need of physical contact right now, but Anthony has never been too keen on public displays of affection. It's understandable with his line of work. Who wants to be able to imagine their doctor groping his girlfriend during their next Pap test or breast exam? Awkward! I shudder at the thought. Consequently, I've learned to expect a discrete amount of physical distance from him in public places.

Kitty shows up with our wine and pours a little into Anthony's glass for sampling. As she waits for Anthony to taste the wine, she gives him a flirty smile and he winks back at her. Satisfied with our selection, Anthony nods to the waitress and she fills up my glass. She then turns to fill up Anthony's glass, leaning over too much and giving him a *second* eye-level view of her boobs.

"Let me know if you need anything else." The waitress says directly to Anthony, biting her bottom lip and practically undressing him with her eyes before she walks away. I choke on my wine. Coughing, I look incredulously back at Anthony, hoping he's as outraged as I am, but find him ogling her rear end as she walks away. What the hell!? I slap him on the shoulder with the back of my hand.

"Ow! What's wrong, babe? You look troubled." Anthony grumpily rubs his shoulder where I slugged him. It wasn't that hard of a slap.

"Uh, you're flirting with Kitty, that's what's wrong!"

TO FLIRT OR NOT TO FLIRT - THAT IS THE CONUNDRUM

6:35 pm

Anthony glances back at our waitress, who's now surrounded by a group of big-breasted hussies, similarly attired in crisp white shirts with the top few buttons undone. They all look in our direction, predatory looks on their faces. Anthony smiles and waves at them, sending them all into a fit of giggles they try to hide by turning their backs to us. Anthony turns back to me and frowns.

"Babe, there's nothing wrong with innocent flirting. It's not like she slipped me her phone number or anything, and that little exchange probably made her night. Not that you'd know, but being a waitress is a really hard job. Customers can be really rude and demanding. Thanks to my flirting, we'll probably get excellent service now. Where's the harm in that?" He takes my hand and gives it a gentle squeeze, before letting it go again. "I'm leaving with you, Gina. That's all that should matter."

"Let me get this straight. You're saying that when you're in a committed relationship it's okay to flirt with someone else as long as the flirting doesn't go anywhere serious?"

"I'd say that's a fair summary of what I said." Anthony takes a sip of his wine, completely unaffected by this topic of discussion.

Now the door is wide open. I wanted to come clean and this is my chance. I can't let this sit any longer. I have too many secrets inside me, and I don't want to keep this one any longer than I have to. My fingers trace the circular base of my wine glass as I muster the courage to start. "Okay, well, remember last Friday night, when Erin and I went out?"

He nods, taking another sip of his wine.

"Well, someone was flirting with me and I've been feeling very awkward about it. I want us to be honest with each other, and the memory has bugged me since it happened."

Anthony puts his glass down and places both palms flat out on the table, as if he's bracing himself for something big.

"Did you sleep with him? Is that what you're trying to tell me, Regina? Are you leaving me?"

"Oh, God! No, nothing like that! It's just

that, well, he was extremely persistent and..." I trail off, unsure what to say.

Anthony's face relaxes and the tension leaves his shoulders.

"Let me guess. You felt flattered and special, and a part of you liked it, but now you're feeling guilty about it, right?"

I nod in shock. That pretty much sums it up—well, except for the part where I realized our sex life is boring and I need more passion in my life.

Anthony continues, "But you didn't sleep with him?"

I shake my head no.

"Then it's a non-issue. I don't know why you're so worried, babe."

Pause. Stop. Rewind. This is not the reaction I was expecting from him.

"So, let me get this straight. If a guy comes on to me and I flirt back but I don't have sex with him, you'd be okay with that?"

"Sure! It's only flirting, Regina. It's harmless fun. You're young and you can't get any prettier. You should be proud men are attracted to you and enjoy it while it lasts. We're only young once. Besides, it's great for my ego, too."

What the hell? He's basically repeating what Pete said, about being young once and taking full advantage of my youth, but it doesn't feel the same when Anthony says it.

"Hold up. How would my flirting with another guy be good for *your* ego?"

"Because it says my girl is so hot other guys want her and she feels confident enough about herself to let it show. See? All good, harmless fun."

I fold my arms across my chest and look at him skeptically. He can't really be okay with any of this, can he?

"Okay, hypothetically speaking, what if the guy kisses me? What then?" I raise my eyebrows, waiting for his answer. Although

Pete never actually kissed me on the lips, he did steal a couple nibbles on my neck.

Anthony's eyebrows furrow, considering my question. "Do you kiss him back?"

"No, I don't kiss him back, I have a boyfriend! I'm not going to kiss some cheeky Casanova back!"

"Again, non-issue. You know you're being faithful. You can't control other people's actions, Regina."

I must be a glutton for punishment, trying to find the guilt in my actions, but I need to make sure I haven't crossed any lines.

"Okay then, Smarty Pants. What if I find him attractive? Let's say I flirt with someone I find very attractive, and he kisses me, but I don't kiss him back. Is that cheating?" I'm trying to find a flaw in his way of seeing things. There is no way this situation can be right.

"Nope. Not cheating at all. You wouldn't

be flirting with him if you didn't find him attractive in the first place, now would you?"

Interesting. I sip my wine, enjoying the fresh crisp taste of it, somewhat relieved that this secret is more or less out in the open. I'm not certain I like his very liberal view on flirting, but maybe this is just more proof that I'm way too uptight, as Erin has so often suggested. Maybe I've been so concerned about keeping to the straight and narrow all my life that I have no definition for innocent flirting.

We sit in silence, me reflecting on our conversation, trying to come to grips with the right and wrong of it all, while Anthony checks his missed text messages. A buxom woman wearing a feminine tuxedo and holding a basket of roses stops near our table. She nods politely to both of us and focuses her attention to Anthony, speaking with a faint French accent.

"Would Monsieur like to purchase a

rose?" Her eyes bounce from Anthony to me, sparkling with the romance of the suggestion. I recall Anthony's jab that serving tables is a hard job I wouldn't understand, and think absently that selling roses to romantic couples sounds like fun. How wonderful to be able to aid in such a sweet gesture. Across the table, Anthony rubs his hands on his pants and looks uncomfortable.

"No, thank you," he answers waving her away. "Maybe another time." Although it would have been romantic—and God knows I could use a little romantic attention from him tonight—I know his financial situation is tight. If my dad weren't picking up the tab for tonight's meal, we wouldn't be in a restaurant like this at all. This restaurant and its accompanying romance are both way out of his price range.

I'M GREEN - AND NOT THE SICKLY KIND

6:56 pm

As if on cue, Daddy arrives with a kiss on the cheek for me and a fatherly clap on the back for Anthony. He sits down and the roses are quickly forgotten.

"Sorry I'm late, but I'm sure you two lovebirds were able to fill in the time. Anthony, I'm glad you could make it to dinner, son. I know what a tight schedule you have. I hope you didn't have too much trouble taking time off of your residency? Regina tells me you've been working double shifts lately." My dad looks at Anthony with all the pride of a future father-in-law.

"Yes, well, considering I've been putting in a lot of hours and my performance has been exemplary, they just couldn't tell me no when I asked for a night off with my best girl." Anthony takes my hand and brings it to his lips for a quick kiss, surprising me at his sudden show of affection in a public place. An uneasy feeling goes through me, as I realize he just told my father a little white lie. Daddy buys it hook, line and sinker, gazing at Anthony with a stupid, almost love-struck smile. Jeez! It's like Anthony is wooing Daddy instead of me!

Anthony scoots his chair closer to mine and drapes his arm along the backrest of my chair, earning yet another appreciative glance from my father. I desperately want to cuddle into his side, but know he'd probably push me away, so I don't. I take in whatever closeness I can get from him for the time being. There will be time for closeness later in the privacy of his apartment.

The woman with the basket of roses passes by our table once more, and Anthony reaches out to stop her. Clearing his throat, Anthony says to the woman, "Excuse me, I'd like to purchase one of your roses."

I put my hand on his arm, thinking he feels guilty about my earlier disappointment, "Anthony, you don't need to buy me a rose."

His eyes bounce from me to my father, "A beautiful flower for a beautiful woman, right?" Dad's eyes light up like he can't believe his luck. Damn! Those two really should be dating each other! But still, it's nice to know that Dad approves of Anthony so much.

Anthony pays the woman and hands me the rose. I try to thank him with a kiss, but he turns his head so that I end up kissing him on the cheek instead.

Dinner progresses smoothly. By the time we reach dessert and espresso, the men are pretty much done talking about the technical aspects of their pet project. I take the opportunity to discuss business of my own and pull out my notes to show Dad. After going over my reports and explaining how money is being squandered uselessly, Dad just shakes his head. Here it comes.

"Princess, don't worry about it. Granz Textiles has more than enough liquidity to cover any additional costs, should they arise."

I should be used to this by now, but I'm a little peeved he disregarded me so quickly. I look at Anthony with an I-told-you-so face and he shrugs his shoulders in response. So much for his earlier conviction that Dad would take my concerns seriously.

"But Dad, with the way our stocks plummeted today, we shouldn't take any financial risks right now. We can't just sell off our assets to fund an experimental project that won't bring in any real profits for a while." I jab my thumb toward Anthony. "I suggest we use..."

Anthony takes my hand and sits up straight. Finally! True to his promise, he's going to take my side and get my dad to listen to me, to take me seriously, and he'll push his own good ideas forward in the process. Hell yeah! Power couple!

"Regina, your father knows Granz Textiles inside and out. If he says there's nothing to worry about, I trust him. Take his advice and use this as a learning experience. You're still very green and have a lot to learn, but the perfect role model to learn from is sitting right in front of you."

Well, fuck me sideways! My head snaps toward him and my jaw drops. He smiles at my dad, who nods his approval to Anthony then pats my hand. He's actually patting my hand! How old am I, two? I'm crushed and stunned into silence. How do I recover from that? There is no way Daddy will take me seriously now. Anthony was supposed to take my side on this, but he belittled me instead. I'm *still very green*?

As if nothing even happened, Dad picks up the bill, Anthony thanks him for his generosity, they man hug, and we all leave the restaurant. I am completely ignored.

I'm fuming as Anthony and I walk from the restaurant toward his apartment. My hands are clenched tightly into fists, and I can feel some of my unhealed wounds cracking open as my nails dig into them.

How could he? He told me he was going to help me get my point across with Dad, but instead he made me sound like I didn't know what the hell I was talking about. Anthony is either completely oblivious to my mood shift or choosing to ignore it, probably blaming it on PMS or something.

I'm way too quiet, and the rapid sound of my heels clicking on the sidewalk only emphasizes how pissed off I am. Pissed is an understatement. Fire hydrants have nothing on me! I just barely refrain from stabbing him with my stilettos.

We pass a newsstand, and my eyes catch a glimpse of a tacky gossip magazine's front page. It's one of those really trashy magazines, where you can usually see blurry UFO pictures and two-headed babies. I don't usually pay attention to those types of magazines, but something draws my attention. This edition boasts a picture of a man with his arms draped around the shoulders of two beautiful women. The bold yellow letters of the headline read, "Pete Ferro scores big with sexy lingerie models." I slow down to read the caption under the picture, "After wreaking havoc at a lingerie fashion show after-party, Pete Ferro leaves with two of the models for his own private demonstration."

Oh, that's just great! Grabbing Anthony's hand a little too roughly, I pick up the pace and walk like a woman on a mission. Lingerie models. Right. Looking down at my own body, I don't wonder why Pete turned me down. So what if my legs aren't long enough to wrap around his hips twice? So what if my breasts are smaller than his fat egotistical head? So what if I'm not seven-feet-tall? Not that I'd even want to wrap my legs around him twice, but the fact that I'm not pretty enough for him stings.

By the time we get into Anthony's apartment, I can't help myself. My anger forgotten, I jump him the instant the front door shuts. Literally. My legs wrap around his hips and my arms wrap around his neck. I press my body as close to his as I can get it with clothes on, kissing him frantically and pulling at our clothes. I'm strung so tight I feel like I'll burst if he doesn't touch me soon.

This is so unlike me but, after the other night with Pete and considering that Anthony and I haven't had sex in over two weeks, I'm hornier than a Viking's helmet. I desperately need an outlet for the passion Pete ignited in me, and that outlet needs to be Anthony. Even if he was a dick over dinner tonight, I know Anthony loves me and I know he's attracted to my body. Lingerie models my ass!

THINGS ARE JUST PURRFECT

JULY 5TH, 4:38 pm

It's Friday afternoon. Restlessness is consuming me, swallowing me whole. Nom, nom, nom, ugh! I tap my toes on the floor, earning annoying glances over the top of my cubicle from my colleagues. I know swirling my pen between my fingers and then rhythmically tapping it three times on my desk is annoying, but I can't help it. This is the better option, considering what I want to do is jump on my desk and scream. My coworkers would have strokes if I did something like that, something that wasn't perfectly proper. Even my panties are proper. No lace, no thongs, and G-strings belong on cellos, not up my ass. The thought makes me giggle. Simon, the guy in the cubicle across from me, scowls at my tapping… again. Well, screw him! I'm too excited about going dancing tonight. I might burst into giggles if I don't fidget.

Erin sent me a text last night, letting me know there is a grand opening tonight up in Port Jeff, a place right on the water. She didn't give much information on the establishment, just that I should "dress for dancing my ass off" and that there would be "hip cats and dolls at the romp," whatever that means.

She loves being cryptic.

My first reaction was, "Hell no!" It's way too soon for partying with her again, maybe ever. But then she mentioned dancing and I was hooked. She also assured me this party would be totally legal.

I'd hoped to see Anthony tonight, but he won't be joining us. The poor guy is always stuck at work.

I think back to the last time I saw him—at his apartment Tuesday morning, the morning after I tried to jump him. How he managed to pry me off is still a mystery. New use for lube: removing your horny girlfriend, you lather up and she slips off.

No, seriously, he wasn't a total ass about it. He shoved me into the shower—alone—under the pretext that I needed to cool off a bit. Okay, maybe he was an ass. I thought he was asking me to freshen up for our little romp in the sack. So I took my time, put my perfume in all the right places, and put on that pale pink glittery lip-gloss he likes, but by the time I got to bed, he was asleep.

I paused a second, staring at him

incredulously, trying not to take it as a personal rejection. So much for my lip-gloss! I had plans for those kisses. Anthony works so hard and really does need his rest.

I was just about to try to sleep unsatisfied, when I remembered a certain pink toy Erin had slipped into my bag as a joke. Desperate, I decided to take care of things solo style. I grabbed the toy from my bag and climbed in bed next to Anthony, hoping he really was sound asleep.

Cautiously, I turned the toy from off to low, the button illuminating the sheets with a faint pink glow. I wiggled the toy this way and that way, but the low vibration of the rabbit shaped toy just wasn't doing it for me. In frustration, I finally blasted the dial to full power. My bad. The overwhelming sensations made me gasp—at least I thought it was a gasp—my eyes closed and rolled back, my vision lost in my wave of bliss. I reflexively arched my back.

"Wow, seriously?" Anthony's voice sounded annoyed. "You woke me up to fuck yourself?"

I, on the other hand, was mortified. I've never done anything like that in front of him—ever! Self-pleasure is not permitted under the rules of our relationship agreement. I looked down, embarrassed, and found the sheet glowing bright pink. My face burned the same shade of pink, and I hastily turned off the toy.

"We made promises, Gina."

"I know, I just miss you and didn't want to wake you up." I tossed the toy on the floor and leaned in toward him, trailing my finger down his bare side. "I'll make it up to you." It was my second offer of the night.

Anthony rolled toward me, his eyes drowsy and angry. My hand slipped from his side. "You've had an endless pile of cash your whole life, so you can't understand. Everything I have, I've worked for. I want to keep you happy, Gina. I want to offer you the same things your family does, and to do that I have to work. Maybe it won't always be this way, but can't you just put aside your carnal urges for a few days, so I can provide for you like I want?"

Guilt is an ugly monster. He looks like a gooey green Cookie Monster, covered in oozing green goo—boogers. He's made of boogers. He's gross, slimy, and all consuming, leaving every inch of my body and heart aching. I never asked Anthony for anything, but regardless he feels threatened by his lack of funds and family connections. He feels he has to work twice as hard to have anyone notice him.

I tugged the blankets up and rolled over. "I'm sorry. I know how hard it is for you. I just wanted—"

With his back to me, he said, "No, you don't have any idea how hard it is to be accepted in your group. They don't accept me, Gina. I have to prove my worth, every damned day. I didn't want to burden you with any of this, but there's more to life than sex."

"And there's more to life than money."

He laughed bitterly, "So says one of the wealthiest women in Manhattan."

I rolled over and put my hand on his shoulder, but he pulled away. "Never mind. Some things are just a certain way, and until I break through that wall, I'm nobody. The day I do, though, everything will change. I will take you to nice places, buy you expensive clothes—"

"I don't want stuff, Anthony. I want you."

He rolled over the rest of the way and looked me in the eye. "You say that now, but if it came to living in a shoebox and wearing Wal-Mart clothes, I don't think you'd like it. I ate Cheerios at every meal for eight months straight, trying to get ahead. I don't want you to make those types of sacrifices. Let me do this and stop worrying. And if you want to break our agreement, about the toys—"

My face turns bright red. "No, we can keep our agreement. No toys, only each other."

"That's my girl." He reached out to cup my cheek. "Wait for me and remember I'm also waiting for you." Then he rolled over and went back to sleep, leaving me with a heavy conscience.

I hate it when he's right. I'm not sure what sparked his no toys rule, but it seemed romantic when I agreed. Then again, we not only had sex more than once a month, we were in the same freakin' room more than once a month. I'm lonely and I miss him so much.

That's probably why Pete got to me. With that realization, I felt better and drifted off to sleep.

PARTY HARDY MARTY

5:58 pm

By the time I finally get home, I'm ready to pull that stick out of my ass and toss it into the South Bay. With my luck, a golden retriever will bring it back.

Cut it out, Gina. Let loose a little bit. I shake out my shoulders and close my eyes. For a moment, I'm someone else, someone who I've buried deep within. I've rarely met her. She's not the ballerina or the perfect child.

She's me.

The corners of my lips twitch into a smile, and I grab a hairbrush. Holding it to my mouth like a microphone, I start singing softly like a little church girl. I take a deep breath, choose a song I can relate to a little too much, and try again.

There are a lot of songs about surviving out there, but this one lights a fire in me. My fingers tighten around my makeshift microphone, and I let the beat course through me, finally letting my outer shell fall away and belting out the lyrics.

I sing as if I don't care if anyone can hear me—the household staff already knows my secret anyway, that I'm less than perfect, that I act like someone I'm not. They also know I'm tone-deaf, one hundred percent, irredeemably tone-deaf. Describing my singing is simple—think of a cat stuck on a weathervane during a tornado. The thought makes me giggle.

That's when my mother barges into my room, as if I'm five-years-old and playing with matches.

"Gina, what on Earth?" Mom trails off, surveying the scene in my bedroom.

I'm wearing only my bra and panties, my hair rolled up in curlers, and a brush by my mouth. The music is blasting and, as she shoves inside my room, awarding her a front row view of my booty-shaking dance moves. Her resulting giggle stops me cold, and I whirl around too fast. The brush goes flying across the room, bounces off the headboard, and smacks into the wall with a thud.

Mom blinks, an amused smile on her face. "I didn't think you liked rap music."

I snatch my robe and pull it on. "It's not rap, Mom. And you could knock. Really."

"Because you might be doing something embarrassing?" She offers a shy smile and walks across my large room. Mom chose the pale blue walls and white trim a few years ago. The raw silk drapes, the velvet headboard, and the antique French armoire—everything was chosen by her. I don't even like blue…unless it's on Pete Ferro. I flinch. Where'd that thought come from?

Mom misinterprets my shiver as annoyance. She sits on my bed and looks up at me. "So you've finally hit your rebellion stage. It's about time."

"It's R&B!"

"I know, but usually when I come in here, you're listening to Chopin and practicing pointe. I'm not used to seeing you in fancy panties, shaking your money-maker." She says it deadpan, without a trace of humor.

My jaw drops and I squawk, "My *money-maker*?"

She raises a single perfect brow, "I've never been certain if that was referring to one's breasts or buttocks. Did I use the expression incorrectly?"

That makes me laugh. She can play this part with Daddy, but not me. I toss a pillow at her. "You know what it means! Buttocks? Really!?"

"By the way, I like those pantyhose with the built-in ass. Tell me, what happens when a guy goes to give you a squeeze and realizes it's stuffed? Most women don't stuff their asses, dear."

"Most daughters don't discuss backdoor matters with their mothers, Mom."

"Touché." She smiles again, but the worry lines between her brows give her away. "Don't get into any trouble. Your father is stressed enough right now, and I'm worried about him. Actually, I'm worried about you. You've been acting different. Is there anything you want to talk about?"

Yes.

"No, Mom. I'm fine. I'm just excited about going dancing with Erin." My mom rolls her eyes at the name. "Come on, she's my best friend and she's making it on her own."

"Is that what you want to do? Leave everything you know behind and abandon all responsibility? What about the people who love her?" Mom is wringing her hands, even though she tries to force her hands into her lap and sit properly on the edge of my bed. Her age shows tonight, especially in her tired eyes.

"Erin's family doesn't—"

"You don't know that," she interrupts. "Love is a strange thing that makes people behave in ways that are otherwise unexplainable." She pauses, rubbing her temples, before continuing. "Gina, I wouldn't wish Erin's life on you for an instant, but if you still feel the need to see what it's like to be her, to go to these places, to be a part of the debauchery that follows your friend around, please, just be careful."

I stiffen at her words. “You don’t think I can handle myself in the real world, is that it? I’m only good if I’m on some wealthy man’s arm, an ornament—is that what you mean?”

“Gina, don’t be silly.” Mom stands and walks over to me. We’re eye to eye. “I’m telling you that I’m here, if you ever want to talk. That’s all. Have fun wearing your fake butt and chicken cutlet boobs.” She tosses the package of cleavage enhancers at me. “For the record, you’re a beautiful woman without those things.” Mom smiles sadly at me, then turns and walks demurely out the door.

I have no words. I’m not sure how she did it, but it feels like she sucked the fun right out of my body. I sit down on the bed, no longer interested in enhancing my curves in all the right places.

THE SEXY CLOWN

9:12 pm

I realize I need tonight to be a release, a way to eliminate the pressure within me, threatening to overtake me with every breath. Even when I close my eyes, it doesn't stop. Nightmares plague me—they're getting worse and harder to hide.

Last night I screamed and sat upright in my bed, covered in sweat and choking from smoke that wasn't there. Pete Ferro didn't save me. The smoke didn't kill me. I was trapped in that hellish room for decades, like it was my own personal Hell.

Someone dressed in solid black, a hood covering his head, finally opened the door. The fire and smoke had no effect on him, probably because the guy was the incarnation of evil.

He pinned me with a wicked smile. His words were simple, "You did this."

My voice is gone, lost long ago. Tears streak down my face as I kneel in front of this guy, hands clasped together, begging him to spare me.

I push the horrid dreams from my mind, trying to shake off the eerie feeling clinging to me. I won't let myself curl up into a ball and panic. Not tonight.

Putting the final touches on my ensemble, I study myself in the mirror one last time, regaining my confidence. My hair is tied in a high ponytail, and my light makeup draws attention to my eyes. A black sleeveless dress with a clingy bodice shows off my natural curves, its swishy skirt brushing the tops of my knees. The neckline of my dress plunges just a little, showing just enough skin, and a narrow red leather belt accentuates my waist. I pull on a pair of red leather T-straps and look in the mirror.

The overall look is very fun and feminine, yet still on the demure side. I would have looked like a pinup if I'd put on my fake curves, but they're still on my bed in their original packaging.

Still, I want something more, some dramatic difference. The old Gina is gone, and this interim Gina scares me. Maybe Erin won't understand. Mother certainly doesn't. I don't feel rebellious, I feel lost. I've always prided myself in being honest and doing what is right. Now those traits are gone, burned to ashes and buried where the warehouse once stood. The warehouse fire marks the end of my old life and the beginning of something else. I don't feel the same anymore. I need a way to visually express the change, but how?

The answer is staring me in the face—a tube of bright red lipstick. I never wear anything so dramatic, so dark. Grabbing a lip pencil, I take my time tracing along the lines of my lips and filling them in. I pick up the tube of red lipstick and paint it carefully in place. When I'm done, I stare in the mirror, not sure if I look sexy or clownish.

The sexy clown. That's a look. My mom is going to think I want to be a rapper, since I'm wearing 'hoochie' lipstick. The thought makes me smile. Screw it. I'm not taking it off or subduing it.

At the sound of the doorbell, I spritz myself with my favorite perfume, pausing to take comfort in a smell I love. So, maybe I can't blame Pete for his obsession with his body wash. It's amazing how a smell can affect your mood in a blink.

I hear Timothy, our butler, and realize that Dad's caught sight of Erin. Those two clash terribly, and if I don't intervene there'll be a brawl.

I hear Daddy's stern deep voice, "How are your parents?"

"Fuck, if I know. How's your patronizing admonition of Gina's choices going? Still the cold-hearted asshole you were before? Or have you realized she has a brain and isn't just your office ornament?"

Holy shit. I'm on the upper landing of the third floor and make my way down the tall winding staircase as fast as possible. If I had on ballet flats I would have run. Damned heels.

"Believe what you want, but I value my daughter. You should return to your parents, Erin, and stop this foolishness. Take your place with your family and stop shaming them with your ludicrous behavior."

I reach the marble foyer floor, my heels clicking sassily, just in time to catch Erin giving Dad the bird. Erin spins around and grins at me. "Holy shit! Look who's hussying it up tonight! You are so going to get laid!"

Dad's face turns red with anger, "Regina Granz, I forbid you to leave my house with this, this—" He's flabbergasted, unable to pull the right words from his mind. The rich have a way of speaking in backhanded insults, and Erin obviously gave that up. Daddy, on the other hand, clings to the way things have been done for generations. There's a proper way to live one's life, a proper way to behave, and Erin is not behaving properly.

Mom shows up at the right time, places her hand on Daddy's arm and smiles at me. "Reginald, our girl knows what is right. She won't get into trouble. Let her go out for a little bit." Mom's smooth tone soothes Daddy's ruffled feathers.

She steps toward me for a hug and whispers in my ear, "If either of you can't drive, be responsible and call for the limo." Erin puffs up, offended, but Mom cuts her off, "I'm not suggesting anyone will have to see you taking a ride in it, but it's better than accidentally killing yourself or someone else. If Gina is your friend, protect her. No drunk driving. Not today, not ever. Use the limo if you need it and stay out of trouble."

Mom leans in and kisses my cheek. She does the same for Erin. It's a gesture that dates back to our childhood. Mom was the mother figure Erin didn't have. Acceptance from Mom means a great deal to her. I can tell because Erin's eyes turn glassy. She stands silently for a moment and then nods.

I admire Erin—a lot. When Erin turned eighteen, she rebelled against her family and their fortune. She became an artist, paying her bills by selling her work in Brooklyn markets and a few Chelsea galleries.

Even though I sometimes envy her, times like this remind me that she's alone. If she can't make it as an artist, her family won't show compassion. One broken bone would make her destitute. One blown transmission, one bad month of sales will force her to crawl back home. She'd rather die than go back home.

I wish I had her backbone, her determination. Erin knows who she is and isn't afraid to speak her mind. Next to her I feel mousy, well, mousy with big red lips.

"Nice look. I nearly died when I heard heels, but when I turned and saw those cherry lips, I thought your dad was going to kill me. I'm sure he's in there blaming me right now."

"Nah, Mom blames you for the purchase of my fake ass and blow-up boobs. Oh, and the rap music. You're such a bad influence." I laugh as we slip into her car.

Erin pulls the door shut and adds, "Yep. I'm a horrible influence making girls with no junk in their trunk buy booty pants. Rich kids everywhere are doomed." She laughs. "Your mom is sweet. I honestly can't tell if she knows stuff or if she's just playing the old lady card to get inside your head."

"Yeah, I'm noticing that too."

We drive the parkway in silence, and I stare at the ocean through the window. Erin still hasn't clued me in on what kind of bar we're going to, and her evasiveness makes me increasingly nervous. My only reassurance is that she's not dressed in any extreme, over the top way. With her skin-tight capri pants and short blouse knotted above her pierced bellybutton, she doesn't look like she dressed for a mosh pit. That's a plus.

After a while, I ask, "So, where are we going? And why are you dressed like Patty Duke?"

Erin glances at me. "Who?"

"I forgot you don't like vintage shows."

"You didn't forget anything. They're called old crap and based solely on a false perception of reality that doesn't even come close to the way people actually live, today or in the past. They're government propaganda and total shit-cake that they want you to swallow with a smile on your face. Sorry, babe. I don't do shit-cake."

"Now you have issues with 'the man?' New phobia?"

"Psh, old news sista'. People with power can't be trusted."

"Which is why you had so much fun ogling the man-beast in action?"

Erin waves a finger at me. "Totally different scenario. That man has money and power, but from a distance he looks normal."

"Yeah, normal. Whatever that is." I study her from the corner of my eye. "Fine, I'll torment you with classic Hitchcock movies some other time, but for now—where are we going? And are you absolutely sure this place is on the up and up? And DAMN it's far away." We're entering the village of Port Jeff.

We park on a crowded side street, and I'm grateful to find we are at least not at a rave. Erin parallel parks and grabs her keys. "Come on, Sherlock. You'll figure it out soon enough. Let's get in line already, so we can have some fun!"

We wander over to a building constructed right on the waterfront. People of all ages are here, some dressed in vintage clothing. I see beautiful outfits ranging from the sleek lines of roaring 20's flapper dresses to the bell curves of the feminine 50's rockabilly dresses.

My body language must be radiating anxiety, because Erin bumps me with her shoulder. Erin hugs me and laughs. "You are just too adorable. You won't get arrested tonight. If you're into that kinky handcuff stuff, though, we can find a way to get you into a bit of sexy trouble." She waggles her eyebrows at me.

"No sexy trouble, Erin. That's only okay if it's Anthony using those handcuffs on me or if I get to use them on him." Did I just say that out loud? I hear people chuckling behind us and my cheeks burn with the realization I may have spoken a bit loudly.

"Hell, yeah! That's my girl! Gina, you and I are going to have so much fun tonight!" She wraps an arm around my shoulders and squeezes me into a half hug, giving my head a companionable bump with hers.

SIT ON MY FACE

10:16 pm

"How did you find out about this place, anyway?" The closer we get to the door, the louder I have to yell for Erin to hear me. The music coming from inside is getting louder, and the crowd by the door is densely packed.

"My downstairs neighbor, Ricky, owns this club," Erin shouts over the crowd. We absently move several steps forward.

I grab Erin's arm and turn her toward me, "Wait, Ricky, as in Oh-My-God-He's-The-Best-Sex-Of-My-Life Ricky?"

"The one and only." She waggles her eyebrows, and we move another step forward.

Eventually, we make it to the front of the line, but a bouncer clicks the red velvet rope back into the metal post, cutting us off. I'm bouncing up and down on the balls of my feet, anxious to get in. My legs feel restless, aching to dance. A night of actual fun, without rules to follow, is long overdue.

I stretch my neck, trying to peek inside, but can't see a thing. Patience is not one of my virtues, especially with The Hulk standing between the dance floor and me. I study the brutish bouncer, in his overly tight t-shirt, his bulging arm muscles stretching the seams. Finally, he puts a hand on his earpiece, nods to someone, and moves the rope, letting us in.

Inside at last, my jaw drops—this place is amazing! The sights, sounds, and smells seem to send me back in time. Ricky has turned an old waterfront house into a retro dance club and bar. Immediately in front of us, a staircase leads to the balcony, where guests seated at tables can watch the dancers below. On the main floor, a beautifully polished wood bar graces one entire wall and hosts an unparalleled assortment of alcoholic beverages. Another wall boasts huge glass doors, through which we have a fantastic view of the water. People pass through the open doors freely, walking along the wrap-around porch and enjoying the cool summer night.

On the third wall, where I expected the typical Friday night rock band to be playing from the stage, a Big Band ensemble of saxophones, trumpets, clarinets and trombones, bop up and down as they play a swing number. Their drummer pounds out rhythms surrounded by a forest of drums, really rounding out that swing beat. A couple dressed in vintage clothing and holding old style microphones croon away at each other in time with the band.

But as much as the atmosphere and the band delight me, it's what I see on the dance floor that makes me swoon. "Erin! They're, they're..." I'm pointing at the dance floor with one hand and tugging on her arm with the other.

"Swing dancing, baby! I knew you'd like it. Come on! Let's get your drink on, and then we'll find you a dance partner."

Erin grabs me by the wrist, pulling me toward the bar. I'm absolutely giddy and can't help being distracted by the other dancers spinning, twirling and rock-stepping.

We weave our way through the crowd, finally securing two stools at the bar. The bartender has his back to us, fixing drinks for other patrons. Erin taps him on the shoulder and he turns around, giving Erin a welcoming smile.

"Hey, Erin! I'm so glad you made it to opening night!" He leans over the bar and gives her an obscene open-mouthed kiss. I turn away, uninterested in seeing my bestie's pierced tongue plunging into some guy's mouth.

The bartender is on the short side, a little older than me, maybe late twenties, with dark hair, dark eyes, and tanned skin. He's dressed in a white button-down shirt with the sleeves rolled halfway up his forearms, high-waist trousers, and suspenders. A chain hangs out of one of his pockets, probably securing a pocket watch, and a fedora hat sits jauntily on top of his head. The outfit is phenomenal. He looks like he just stepped out of the 1940's.

When they stop sucking face, I hear Erin huskily say, "Wouldn't miss this for anything! Hey, Ricky! This is my friend, Gina."

Ricky looks my way, and I extend a hand. "It's nice to finally meet you. This place is amazing, congrats!"

"Thanks! It's great to finally meet you too, Gina. I've heard so much about you," he says smiling as if he means it.

"Ditto," I blush. I think about the things I've heard about Ricky… well, let's just say he may be short in height, but Erin is all praise when it comes to his other attributes.

"Hey, Ricky, Gina is in need of a dirty drink and a good dance partner. Or a good drink and a dirty dance partner, whichever we can find first. Can you help us out?"

"Yep! I'm on it, doll. Just let me get these customers taken care of, and I'll be right back."

I give Erin a half-hearted embarrassed slap on the shoulder. Laughing, Ricky knocks his knuckles on the bar and returns to his other patrons.

Erin and I turn around on our stools to face the rest of the room. The atmosphere is festive, the music is lively, and the dancing...oh, the dancing! It's carefree and wild.

I watch an obviously more experienced couple do lifts and throws; the girl looks positively weightless and the guy beams with the excitement of each new step. The floor clears around them, providing room for them to show off their moves. Their audience claps their hands to the beat of the live band's music, everyone laughing, whistling, or cat calling as the couple cuts a rug.

Some less experienced dancers loiter off to the side, still trying to figure out basic steps, stepping on each other's toes, and bumping foreheads, but laughing at their own failed attempts. Watching them, I'm hit with a sudden urge to want to learn *everything*—every step, every spin, and every throw. I want, no, I need to be good at this. I always wanted to learn how to swing dance, but my parents were adamant I stick to ballet and nothing else.

I feel a tap on my shoulder, and both Erin and I turn around, facing the bar once more. Ricky has returned, still behind his bar, and he's gesturing to two shot glasses on the bar in front of us.

"Ladies, Sit on My Face."

Shocked, I turn to Erin. He did NOT just suggest that, did he? The look on my face must be quite something, because they both burst out laughing.

"Relax, Gina. It's the name of the drink, not an invitation." Erin takes her glass, tosses its contents back, and slams it back down on the bar.

Well, here goes nothing. I take my own glass and throw back its contents, surprised when the brownish concoction goes down smoothly. It's strong, sweet, and absolutely delicious. Despite how good it tastes, though, there is no way I am ever going to order that drink by name—ever! Ricky startles me with a loud clap of his hands, and I jump, shocked out of my thoughts.

"Okey-dokey, ladies, time to dance! I have Ted covering the bar for the next song, so who's my lucky lady?" He rubs his hands together, and Erin takes my wrist, pulling my arm above my head.

"Gina goes first!" She says all too quickly. Ricky puts both hands on the bar, and before I know it, he's airborne, jumping over the bar toward our side.

I lean in toward Erin, "Is this guy for real?"

Instead of answering me, she pushes me toward my dance partner. He takes my hand, and we make our way to the dance floor. I'm starting to get a tad nervous, because this is so new to me, but excitement overpowers my nerves and all I want to do is dance.

"So, you ever swing dance before, Gina?" Ricky yells over the music, as he pulls us to a spot close to the center of the dance floor. I straighten my shoulders and lift my chin, trying to be brave, even though I don't know what the heck I'm doing.

"Never. I apologize ahead of time for any bodily harm inflicted. I'm a ballerina, not a Charleston chick."

Ricky laughs and pulls me into the proper position. "Well, by the time I'm done with you, you'll be both."

Patiently, Ricky teaches me the basic rock-step, turns, and how to dip. We pick up speed as I get the hang of it, which doesn't take long. All styles of dance share basic concepts, it's just a matter of learning the steps that make that style unique.

By the end of the song, we're going fast enough to break out in a sweat, and my blood is pumping rapidly in my veins. When the band stops for a break, everyone around us applauds. Ricky kisses the back of my hand and bows his head.

"You're a natural! I have to get back to the bar. I'll get you gals another drink. Come on!" He jogs all the way to the bar and jumps over it again to get back to his workstation.

Erin is sitting on her barstool, waiting for us and beaming. "That was swicked cool, Gina! I can totally see you dancing like that other couple over there." She points to the really good couple from earlier, the couple that had been doing all the impressive throws and lifts. Erin's smile is contagious and suddenly I'm smiling, too.

"This is so much fun, Erin. Thank you so much for bringing me here!"

We hug, but are interrupted by a low voice asking, "Sit on My Face?"

Erin and I part from our hug to see

Ricky, looking like a lost puppy with big eyes and pouty lips, trying to make his way into our little moment. He's also handing us each another shot. Erin and I look at each other and burst into uncontrollable laughter.

YOLO & THE ASS-GRABBER

11:28 pm

The night goes on, Ricky alternating between his bartending duties—during which we are treated to more of his naughty shots—and dancing with Erin or me. His stellar teaching abilities and the large quantities of alcohol in my system work together, loosening me up and making me more daring as we progress into more difficult moves.

During one of these moves, Ricky throws my hands down and tells me to bend over and tuck my arms under my legs. He leans forward over my back, grabs my hands and before I know it, he's flipping me over, making me do a summersault in the air and landing facing him. The feeling is exhilarating! We repeat the move a couple more times during the song, and it becomes increasingly fluid.

The alcohol has definitely taken over, because, when the song is over, I try my best to meet Erin at the bar, but tables and chairs appear in my way as if by magic. It's funny how the alcohol doesn't impair my dancing, but when I try to walk in a straight line I'm a real hazard. Erin is doubled over with laughter on her barstool.

"Ha! That was awesome, Gina! Your Mom would shit her knickers if she saw you flashed your underwear like that! Nice panties, by the way. I never knew you had such a perky ass." Though I could never admit it, I'm suddenly grateful to my mother for discouraging me from wearing the padded pantyhose.

Erin is holding her side, as if she has a stitch from all the laughter. My logic thinks maybe I should be mortified by Erin's comments, but I can't figure out why. Everything just feels so fuzzy and warm and happy. I start to crack up and I can't stop. Erin and I both take a deep breath at the same time, trying to stop laughing, but when we look at each other, we both explode into laughter again.

I'm bent over my stool, unable to stop laughing and unable to remember why I'm laughing in the first place. My world momentarily spins a bit too fast, and I end up on the floor, on my ass, my skirt hiked up to an indecent level. Oh! That's right! I was laughing over showing everyone my panties. Oh, what the hell, I've already flashed all of these people anyway. Erin gets a worried look on her face for all of thirty seconds, before she sees I'm fine and bursts into another fit of giggles. Yeah, we're not driving ourselves home tonight. I manage to stand up and fix my skirt before sitting back down on my stool.

"You know what, Erin? To hell with it! Why should I care who saw my ass? I had fun, damn it! This is my life, and I'll do with it what I bloody well please. Besides, I've been told life is too short to hold back."

"Oh, hell yeah, Gina! YOLO, carpe diem and all that crap, baby girl! Now all we need to do is to get you to fly out of Mommy and Daddy's nest. What do you say? Move in with me. I need a roommate, and you're way too old to be living at your folk's house anyway. C'mon. It'd be great. Please say yes!"

This isn't the first time Erin has brought up the subject of our moving in together.

When she left home, I couldn't fathom why anyone would be in a hurry to leave the comfort of the family mansion. It's not like we are hurting for space, at least not until recently. Over the past week, it seems like my family's house gets smaller each day.

All that space and there is still nowhere I can go to just be me. Each room of the house somehow reminds me who I'm supposed to be, what is expected of me, and how I haven't lived up to their expectations. My father's voice echoes through the halls as he yells at detectives and lawyers, complaining about all the claims coming in from the injured, constantly reminding me of all the harm I've done to so many people. I feel myself spiraling back into my dark pit of remorse. The past week has been nothing but endless attempts at climbing out of that pit, only to be tossed back in again.

A painful grip on my chin jerks me back

to the here and now. Erin searches my eyes, then slaps her hand on the bar and yells, "Ricky, we need another round pronto!" Her eyes never leave mine, but when she speaks again she lowers her voice. "Listen to me, Gina. I know what you're thinking and you need to stop it right now. It wasn't your fault. Do you hear me? You are not the one who started that fire." The hand holding my chin slides up to squeeze my cheeks, making me look like a fish. She grins and adds, "Damn, you look sexy like that… is that Botox?" My eyes open wide, and we both explode into another fit of laughter. Ricky hands us our shots.

No sooner do I slam my glass back down onto the bar, than a man walks up to us. He's fairly nice looking, tall with dark hair, and I judge him to be in his early thirties, though it's hard to say for sure in the dim lighting. He's wearing jeans and a t-shirt instead of the vintage swing clothes most of the people here are wearing. He extends a hand to me and asks, "Would you like to dance?"

Of course, my first thought is "I have a boyfriend," but my new self insists one dance won't hurt. Live! Laugh! Have fun! YOLO! Carpe diem!

"Sure!" I take the guy's hand and we head toward the dance floor.

The song starts off on the slow side, but quickly picks up and in no time we are rock stepping, turning and dipping smoothly. He's not as experienced a dancer as Ricky is, but he's not bad either. He spins me out, then he spins me in, and when he wraps his arm around me for the next move, I feel his hand on my butt cheek, instead of on my lower back. Removing my hand from his shoulder, I slide his obtrusive hand back up to where it's supposed to be. He tries the move one more time, placing his most unwelcome hand on my ass, and I firmly slide it up on my lower back again. The guy is really starting to get on my nerves. There's harmless flirting and then there's repetitive ass grabbing. I'm pretty sure this crosses the line.

We go for a dip and he takes a lick at my neck. All right, that's enough! After he straightens me from the dip, he spins me in close to him only to spin me back out again. I'm anticipating his next move, and there is no way he's going to enjoy it. As soon as my arm reaches full extension, he's going to snap me back into him and my knee will be ready to meet his junk. I smirk at my plan and can't wait to see the look on his face when I do it.

To my surprise, he miscalculates his spin and I end up smacking my face into a wall —a warm, yummy-smelling wall. Since when do walls have arms? This wall has arms, and they are wrapped around me tightly. I feel Ass-Grabber release my hand

and I look up. I don't know if I want to smile like an idiot or push away. Blue eyes look down at me, and a beautiful mouth turns up into a wicked grin.

It's Pete, and he's even more beautiful than I remembered him being, if that's possible.

That sinful voice penetrates the noise, making my stomach flip. "Mind if I cut in?"

COMING SOON:

LIFE BEFORE DAMAGED 3
THE FERRO FAMILY

*****

To ensure you don't miss H.M. Ward's next book, text AWESOMEBOOKS (one word) to 22828 and you will get an email reminder on release day.

*****

Want to talk to other fans?
Go to Facebook and join the discussion!

MORE FERRO FAMILY BOOKS

NICK FERRO

~THE WEDDING CONTRACT~

*****

BRYAN FERRO

~THE PROPOSITION~

*****

SEAN FERRO

~THE ARRANGEMENT~

******

PETER FERRO GRANZ

~DAMAGED~

******

JONATHAN FERRO

~STRIPPED~

******

MORE ROMANCE BY H.M. WARD

SCANDALOUS

SCANDALOUS 2

SECRETS

THE SECRET LIFE OF TRYSTAN SCOTT

DEMON KISSED

CHRISTMAS KISSES

SECOND CHANCES

And more.

To see a full book list, please visit:
www.sexyawesomebooks.com/#!/BOOKS

CAN'T WAIT FOR H.M. WARD'S NEXT STEAMY BOOK?

★★★★★

Let her know by leaving stars and telling her what you liked about

LIFE BEFORE DAMAGED 2

in a review!

COVER REVEAL:

18874463R00077

Made in the USA
San Bernardino, CA
02 February 2015